HILDA
HEN'S
HAPPY
BIRTHDAY

For Lucy and Graham

MARY WORMELL

HILDA HEN'S HAPPY BIRTHDAY

VOYAGER BOOKS
HARCOURT BRACE & COMPANY
San Diego   New York   London
Printed in Hong Kong

It was a lovely sunny morning, and
Hilda Hen wondered if anyone had
remembered it was her birthday.
First she went to the horse's stable.

"Just look," clucked Hilda.
"The horse has left me
some oats. How nice."

She quickly gobbled them up.

The horse arrived back from her morning gallop.
"Oh, the oats!" snorted the horse.
"Lovely," clucked Hilda.
"Thank you so much."

And she went on her way.

"Just look," clucked Hilda.
"The gardener has left me
some apples. How kind."

She eagerly pecked at the apples.

The gardener looked down.
"Oh, the apples," she sighed.
"Lovely," clucked Hilda.
"Thank you so much."

And she went on her way.

"Just look," clucked Hilda.
"The farmer's wife has made
me a dust bath."

She hurriedly scraped the flowers
out of the way.

The farmer's wife arrived with her
watering can.
"Oh, the flower bed," she wailed.
"Lovely," clucked Hilda.
"Thank you so much."

And she went on her way.

"Just look," clucked Hilda.
"The farmer has left me some
tea and cookies. My favorites."

She happily drank the tea
and pecked at the cookies.

The farmer reached out for his tea.
"Oh, the tea and cookies," he cried.
"Lovely," clucked Hilda.
"Thank you so much."

And she went on her way.

"Just look," clucked Hilda.
"My friends have set the table for
my birthday party. How wonderful."

She jumped up onto the table. All the other hens joined her, and Otto, the rooster, crowed, "Cock a doodle-do! Happy birthday to you!"

They all pecked contentedly at the crumbs. And Hilda Hen clucked, "Thank you, everyone, for my presents. I've had a really happy birthday."

First published in Great Britain 1995 by
Victor Gollancz
Copyright © Mary Wormell 1995

Requests for permission to make copies
of any part of the work should be mailed to:
Permissions Department,
Harcourt Brace & Company,
6277 Sea Harbor Drive,
Orlando, Florida 32887-6777.

Library of Congress Cataloging-in-Publication Data
Wormell, Mary.
Hilda Hen's happy birthday/Mary Wormell.
p. cm.
"First published in Great Britain in 1995
by Victor Gollancz"—T.p. verso.
Summary: Hilda Hen finds birthday presents
even in places her farm friends didn't intend.
ISBN 0-15-200299-5   ISBN 0-15-200777-6 (pbk.)
[1. Chickens—Fiction.
2. Birthdays—Fiction.   3. Farm life—Fiction.
4. Domestic animals—Fiction.]   I. Title.
PZ7.W88774Hg 1995
[E]—dc20   94-21020

The text and display type was set in Bramley Medium.

A B C D E   A B C D E (pbk.)